DREA

"What ma[...] anyone wants t[...]ittle freak carnival ru[...]oser friends?" Amy slowly [...] other students in the room "Any[...]" – she placed a not so subtle empha[...] on the word – "will definitely want to come to the fashion show. That's why I'm definitely going ahead with it whether our treasurer agrees with me or not." She smirked. "Call it a presidential decree."

It wasn't easy to make Sam angry. Even when all his friends were totally ticked off about something, he was usually the one who stayed calm and rational.

But this was too much. What gave Amy Anderson the right to decide what was best for everyone else?

"Fine," he said. His voice came out sounding as cold as Amy's. "Do what you want, Ms. President. But I'm definitely going ahead with the school fair. And you can call *that* whatever you want."

M·a·k·i·n·g F·r·i·e·n·d·s

All *Making Friends* titles can be ordered at your local bookshop or are available by post from Book Service by Post (tel: 01624 675137).

Making Friends

Dream on, Amy

Kate Andrews

MACMILLAN CHILDREN'S BOOKS

First published 1998 by Macmillan Children's Books
a division of Macmillan Publishers Limited
25 Eccleston Place, London SW1W 9NF
and Basingstoke

Associated companies throughout the world

ISBN 0 330 36933 4

Copyright © Dan Weiss Associates, Inc. 1998
Photography by Jutta Klee

The right of Kate Andrews to be identified as the
author of this work has been asserted by her in accordance
with the Copyright, Designs and Patents Act 1988.

All rights reserved. No part of this publication may be reproduced, stored in or
introduced into a retrieval system, or transmitted, in any form, or by any means
(electronic, mechanical, photocopying, recording or otherwise) without the prior
written permission of the publisher. Any person who does any unauthorized act in
relation to this publication may be liable to criminal prosecution and civil claims for
damages.

1 3 5 7 9 8 6 4 2

A CIP catalogue record for this book is available from
the British Library

Printed and bound in Great Britain by Mackays of Chatham plc, Kent

This book is sold subject to the condition that it shall not,
by way of trade or otherwise, be lent, re-sold, hired out,
or otherwise circulated without the publisher's prior consent
in any form of binding or cover other than that in which
it is published and without a similar condition including this
condition being imposed on the subsequent purchaser.

The cast of
M·a·k·i·n·g F·r·i·e·n·d·s

Alex

Age: 13

Looks: Light brown hair, blue eyes

Family: Mother died when she was a baby; lives with her dad and her brother Matt, aged 14

Likes: Skateboarding; her family and friends; wearing baggy T-shirts and jeans; being adventurous; letting her feelings show!

Dislikes: People who make fun of her skateboard, her brother or her dad; dressing smart or girly; anything to do with maths or science; dishonesty

Carrie

Age: 13

Looks: Long dark hair – often dyed black! Hazel eyes

Family: Awful! No brothers or sisters; very rich parents who go on about money all the time

Likes: Writing stories; wearing black (drives her mum mad!); thinking deep thoughts; Sky's parents and their awesome houseboat!

Dislikes: Her full name – Carrington; her parents; her mum's choice of clothes; jokes about her hair; computers

Sky

Age: 13

Looks: Light brown skin, dark hair, brown eyes

Family: Crazy! Lives on a houseboat with weird parents and a brother, Leif, aged 8

Likes: Shopping; trendy gear; TV; pop music; talking!

Dislikes: Her parents' bizarre lifestyle; having no money; eating meat

Jordan

Age: 13

Looks: Floppy fair hair, green eyes

Family: Uncomfortable! Four big brothers – all so brilliant at sports he can never compete with them

Likes: Drawing! (especially cartoons); basketball (but don't tell anyone!); playing sax (badly); taking the mickey out of his brothers

Dislikes: Being "baby brother" to four brainless apes; Sky when she starts gossiping

Sam

Age: 13

Looks: Native-American; very dark hair, very dark eyes

Family: Confusing! Both parents are Native-American but have different views on how their kids should look and behave; one sister – Shawna, aged 16

Likes: Skateboarding with Alex; computers (especially surfing the Net); writing for the school paper; goofing around

Dislikes: The way his friends dump their problems on each other; his parents' arguments

Amy

Age: 13

Looks: Sickeningly gorgeous blonde hair; baby blue eyes (yuck!)

Family: Spoilt rotten by her dad, which worries her mum; two big sisters

Likes: Having loads of expensive clothes; making other people feel stupid; Matt (Alex's brother) – she fancies him; being leader of "The Amys" – her bunch of snobby friends

Dislikes: Alex, Carrie and Sky! Looking stupid or childish

Mel

Age: 13

Looks: Black hair, dark eyes

Family: Nice parents who work very hard to do their best for Mel

Likes: Her mum and dad; her friends – but should these be the Amys, or Alex, Carrie and Sky? Standing up for herself; reading horror novels

Dislikes: Amy, when she's rotten to other people; worrying about who are her *real* friends

Sam Wells's
Political Diary

I _knew_ I was born to be a politician!

Ever since I won the election for treasurer of Robert Lowell Middle School, I've been having a total blast. Okay, so it hasn't really been all that long since the election. Still, we've had a few meetings of the new student council already. And at the last one Principal Cashen hit us with a challenge: to think up a fund-raiser to collect the major cash we'll need if we want to have a school trip this year. It only took me about ten seconds to come up with an amazingly awesome plan.

Actually it's not such a totally

new idea. It's something I kicked around a little during my campaign. So in a way that makes it even better. My friends, especially Carrie, kept telling me that all the wild stuff I was telling people I'd do when I was elected was just <u>proposals</u>, not promises. But it still kind of bugged me to talk about stuff I wasn't sure I'd be able to pull off. I guess it's true what Carrie and Jordan and the rest of them are always saying: I can be a little too straight-and-narrow for my own good sometimes.

Anyway, my friends and I spent all afternoon planning how I should tell the rest of the student council about my idea at tomorrow's meeting. We decided I should have a bunch of specifics worked out first; that way it will be easier to convince everyone that my idea will fly. Not that I'm sweating that one too much.

But being prepared is important, so the five of us talked it out the whole way home on the bus yesterday, and then we hung out on Sky's houseboat and talked some more. I even managed to choke down a few of the tofu-and-carob brownies Sky's mom and dad offered us in between their chants. Man, I don't know how Sky survives on that kind of peace-and-love hippie food.

There's just one thing that's bumming me out a little. Namely the thought of putting my idea out there in front of The Amys tomorrow. Amy Anderson and Aimee Stewart still aren't exactly thrilled that I beat out the third member of their group, Mel Eng, in the election. The three of them take being the most popular girls in school pretty seriously. It's like their main purpose in life. And since Amy and Aimee are president and vice president of the student council, they've had plenty of chances to remind me that I'm not their number-one favorite guy on earth right now. They're always ragging on me during meetings and making snide little comments about me and my friends.

I'm used to that. They rag on everybody about everything. I just hope that this time, it doesn't get in the way of my cool idea and ruin things for the whole school.

One

Amy Anderson lingered in front of the girls'-room mirror for one last moment. She pulled a few strands of her long blond hair forward so they hung across her forehead and studied the effect. It looked awfully good. *Then again, when do I ever* not *look good?* Amy asked herself with satisfaction.

"Come on, Amy," Aimee Stewart said anxiously, glancing at her watch. Her round face ringed with blond curls wore an anxious expression. "We're going to be late for the meeting."

Mel Eng screwed the top back on her lip gloss. "What are you worried about, Aimee?" she joked. "It's not like they're going to start without you."

"No kidding," Amy agreed, shooting Aimee a slightly irritated glance.

She had realized long ago that Aimee

5

wasn't what you would call a major thinker. Sometimes she could get caught up in stupid details, like getting to meetings on time, and totally miss the big picture. Still, Amy reminded herself, she was a good friend and unquestionably loyal.

"Anyway, I'm ready now," Amy went on, brushing her hair back from her face again and turning away from the mirror. "Let's go, Aimee. Later, Mel."

"Have fun," Mel replied, pulling a small tortoiseshell comb out of her purse and turning back to the mirror.

Amy and Aimee left the girls' room and strolled down the hall toward Mr. Tate's classroom, where the meeting was being held. The school day had just ended, and the halls were bustling with fifth, sixth, seventh, and eighth graders. With every step Amy took, she saw kids pause to smile at her and Aimee, or say hi, or just watch them walk by. That was the magic of The Amys. And Amy knew that she could take most of the credit for it.

It had started at the beginning of the fifth grade. From the moment Amy

Anderson had set foot in Robert Lowell Middle School, she had known she was going to leave her mark on the place. It was practically her destiny.

Since then she had learned that it really wasn't hard to make people worship you—not if you were blessed with amazing good looks and a personality that practically oozed cool. People were so predictable, really. You just had to know their weaknesses. That's what her father always said. And he obviously knew what he was talking about—after all, he was the chief executive of a very successful financial company with a gigantic, luxurious office overlooking all of downtown Seattle.

Amy had learned a lot by watching the way her father dealt with people. She had also picked up a few tricks from her mother. Mrs. Ayers-Anderson was used to getting what she wanted. That was why she made so much money as a lawyer.

Amy always got what she wanted, too. All The Amys did, thanks to her. Especially now that they were eighth graders—the rulers of the school. It was practically a law of nature.

As she and Aimee sauntered into Mr. Tate's room Amy saw Sam Wells glance up with a frown. He was slouched into a desk near the windows, across the aisle from the sixth-grade representative. "Glad you two could make it," he mumbled.

"What*ever*," Aimee snapped.

But Amy didn't bother to respond. Until recently she had never felt strongly one way or the other about Sam. On the plus side he was kind of cute—dark eyes, dark spiky hair, an adorable lopsided smile. Plus he was a pretty good skateboarder, and he could do a wicked imitation of Principal Cashen. On the negative side he was best friends with that bunch of losers from Taylor Haven.

"I still can't believe he beat Mel," Aimee muttered as they wove their way to the front of the room. "I didn't think anyone but his loser friends would vote for him."

"I know. Can you say 'fixed election'?"

"Do you really think anyone in his little crowd is smart enough to figure out how to cheat?" Aimee asked with a playful grin.

Amy laughed. "Doubt it."

8

Amy's nose wrinkled in disgust as she thought about Sam's friends. There was Jordan Sullivan, self-appointed class clown, with his silly scribbles that he called cartoons, which Principal Cashen was always forcing her to include in the school paper. Then there was Alex Wagner, who was so totally obsessed with skateboarding that she apparently hadn't yet noticed she was a girl instead of a boy. And that hyper tree-hugging teenybopper Skyler Foley. She and her hippie parents actually lived on a *boat*. Hello! What decade were *they* living in? And who could forget Amy's personal *least*-favorite person in school, that ridiculous goth-rock freak Carrie Mersel, with her all-black wardrobe and her stringy dyed black hair?

"Of course, there are those total silicon lepers Sam hangs out with in the computer lab," Amy said as she stepped over a stray backpack. "Even Carrie looks like a social superstar next to those dorks."

"You're right. The Inter-nerds probably could've stuffed the ballots," Aimee agreed.

"The boy just has no taste in people," Amy said. "It's a shame, really."

Until recently The Amys had mostly ignored Sam. But all that had changed now. Sam had dared to challenge The Amys in the school election—and worse yet, he had won.

But Amy was about to remind Sam exactly who was in charge of this school. And it was going to be easy. All she had to do was reveal her incredible plan for the school fund-raiser. Even Sam Wells wouldn't be able to fight that.

Mr. Tate was sitting at the back of the room with his ruddy, bearded face buried in *The Seattle Times*. Technically speaking, the tall, burly science teacher was the faculty adviser to the student council. But at the beginning of the first meeting he had told the students that they could run things on their own. He was just there as backup. Since then he hadn't said a word at any of the meetings.

That was just fine with Amy. It meant that as president, she was in charge.

"Okay, everyone," she said, walking over to the large desk at the front of the room as Aimee took a seat in the first row. "Let's get started. We don't have any time to waste if we're going to raise enough money for the school trip."

She paused long enough to make eye contact with every person in the room. The only one who wasn't focusing every ounce of attention on her was Sam—of course. He was looking down at some papers he was holding. Amy stared at him until he looked up.

Then she smiled sweetly and continued. "As you all know, we have absolutely no cash in the student council budget right now, which means we have our work cut out for us. Luckily I think I have just the answer."

"What is it, Amy?" Krysta Barton, the seventh-grade rep, asked eagerly. Krysta was leaning forward in her seat, her reddish brown bangs falling into her eyes as usual.

Amy forced herself to smile at Krysta. She didn't like the little poser—Krysta was always sucking up to her and then telling her little seventh-grade friends that she was close, personal friends with The Amys. One of these days Amy would have to put Krysta in her place. But she didn't want to upset anyone right now. She was counting on unanimous support for her idea.

"This fund-raiser," Amy said dramatically, "is probably going to be the biggest thing ever to hit Robert Lowell Middle School. It's guaranteed to raise all the cash we need and more." She paused again. Timing was everything. She didn't go on until she could see her audience practically drooling with anticipation.

Then she smiled and dropped her bombshell. "We're going to put on our very own fashion show!"

Two

Sam could hardly believe his ears. A fashion show? What kind of lame idea was that?

He glanced around the room and noticed that he seemed to be alone in his opinion. Everybody else was chattering excitedly about The Amys' announcement. Krysta Barton even applauded. And Amy had that familiar confident, self-satisfied smirk on her face as she ate up the reaction.

Sam shook his head. The Amys never failed to amaze him. A fashion show was so typical. It was shallow, silly, and ridiculous. More important, it was guaranteed *not* to appeal to half the student body—namely the boys.

And some of the girls, too, Sam reminded himself. *I can't exactly see Carrie rushing to ooh and aah at the latest winter fashions. Or Alex, either. Not unless the models skateboard down the catwalk!*

He glanced around the room again. The other kids were practically falling all over each other to tell Amy how fabulous her idea was.

Sam sighed. There was no question about it—it was up to him to bring some sense back to the proceedings.

"Okay, it sounds like everyone's in favor," Amy said. "But just to be official about this, let's take a vote. All in favor, say—"

"Wait," Sam broke in. "I think we need to discuss some more ideas first."

He stood and walked to the front of the room. Amy watched his approach with her blue eyes narrowed suspiciously.

"What are you talking about?" she demanded. "Everyone is crazy about my idea. And there's a good reason for that. It totally rocks. So what's to discuss?"

"She's right," Aimee chimed in.

Sam rolled his eyes. Big surprise there. The Amys all backed each other up. But Aimee was practically Amy's echo. Sam's friend Jordan Sullivan, who was always drawing cartoons and caricatures of people, had once done a cartoon where

Aimee was a big, fashionably dressed parrot perched on Amy's shoulder. It had captured their personalities perfectly.

"I just think we should consider the pros and cons of this fashion show thing," Sam said evenly. He glanced at the fifth-grade rep, a skinny boy named Eddie Rodriguez. "Eddie, man, are you honestly excited about watching a bunch of models prance around in overpriced clothes?"

Eddie had been gazing at Amy in awe. His eyes seemed to be focused somewhere around the neighborhood of her belly button, which was proudly displayed between the bottom hem of her cropped baby T-shirt and the top of her skintight miniskirt. Now Eddie tore his gaze away long enough to give Sam a sheepish look. "Well . . . I dunno," he mumbled. "It could be sort of interesting, maybe. . . ."

Sam turned away from Eddie. He had his attention now—and everybody else's, too. But he knew he probably only had a few seconds to talk some sense into them before they were totally swept away on a tide of Amy worship.

"Listen," he said, "before we jump to a

decision, let's give everyone a chance to speak. I'm sure we all have some great ideas to kick around." *Especially me*, he added to himself. His idea was definitely better than a stupid fashion show. Even these Amy-crazed reps were sure to recognize that.

Krysta raised her hand. "I think a fashion show is a fantastic idea," she announced.

Aimee smirked at Amy, then turned to Sam. "See?" she sneered, tossing her blond curls triumphantly. "Everyone except you loves this idea."

"Right," Amy added. "Why don't you just be mature for once and give in gracefully?"

Sam ignored them. "How about you, Eddie?" he prompted. He was eager to share his idea. But unlike Amy and her zombie followers, he understood that the student council was supposed to be a group effort. He wanted to make sure everyone had a chance to speak up. "Did you come up with any fund-raising ideas?"

The younger boy blushed. "Um, I didn't really think of anything," he said. "Except maybe a skateboard rally or a basketball tournament or something like that."

Sam forced himself not to sigh in exasperation. One of the things he was discovering about politics was that most people were just out for their own interests. The Amys. Eddie. Even his own friends—like when Sky suggested spending the class money on improving the cafeteria's vegetarian lunches. Sometimes Sam thought he was the only one who really wanted to make things better for everyone.

"Okay, a sports event is a possibility," he said tactfully. "But I've got another idea to throw out there. What if we held a school fair?"

He caught a glimpse of Amy and Aimee rolling their eyes at each other, but he continued without missing a beat. That was one thing the election had taught him—if he wanted to get things done, he couldn't let The Amys intimidate him.

"It could be on a Saturday," he said. "All the kids in school can participate to set up different booths and events and stuff."

He quickly glanced down at the sheet of notebook paper he was holding. As he scanned the list he and his friends had made, he felt himself getting psyched all over again. The fair was an amazing idea. No question about it.

"My friends and I were talking," he went on, pacing back and forth at the front of the room, "and we came up with some ideas for activities and stuff. Sky Foley's mom said she would tell astrological fortunes, and Carrie Mersel can get her mom's country club to run pony rides or something like that. You've all seen Jordan Sullivan's cartoons in the school paper— he offered to do caricatures. Alex Wagner suggested a dunking booth." He grinned. "Even Brick—he's the bus driver for bus number four, for those of you who don't know him—wants to pitch in. He's in a really awesome rock band, and he said they'd play for free."

Sam decided not to go into any further detail. There would be plenty of time to explain some of the more technical stuff, like how Alex's father, who had worked on advertising campaigns for lots of local businesses, could contact his clients to help out and donate their services. Or how the kids could offer advertising space on posters or in the school paper in exchange for free food and supplies from area restaurants and caterers. Right now he just wanted to get everybody on board. To make them all see that the fair was an event the whole school could get behind and have fun with.

"That sounds pretty cool." Eddie spoke up tentatively.

Krysta started to nod. Then she glanced at Amy and stopped herself. She shrugged instead. "I don't know," she said. "I still think the fashion show would be better."

The sixth-grade rep spoke up for the first time. She was a smart girl named Janine Waite. Sam didn't know her very well yet, but he already liked her. She didn't waste words—much like Sam himself. "I like Sam's idea," Janine said bluntly. "It would be more fun for more people. Not everybody is interested in fashion."

"Maybe not," Aimee shot back. "But maybe certain people *should* be." She let her gaze run slowly and deliberately over Janine's straight black hair, wire-rimmed glasses, and cotton jumper.

Janine blushed. "That's your opinion," she said hotly. "I think the fair would make more money."

"That's probably true," Eddie put in. "Even little kids could come to a fair."

Aimee sniffed. "Oh, please," she said. "Who needs a bunch of whining little brats, anyway? They don't have any money."

Janine looked unconvinced. "Their parents, do, though," she pointed out.

The debate raged on for a few minutes, with each representative offering opinions and suggestions on both ideas. Sam smiled. This was more like it. They could talk it out until they agreed on the best idea—namely his.

He turned to see how Amy was taking it all. She was standing there with her arms crossed, glaring at him.

"What makes you think, Sam," she said coldly, bringing all other discussion in the room to an immediate halt, "that anyone wants to come to a pathetic little freak carnival run by you and your loser friends?" She slowly surveyed the other students in the room. "Anyone *cool*"—she placed a not so subtle emphasis on the word—"will definitely want to come to the fashion show. That's why I'm definitely going ahead with it whether our treasurer agrees with me or not." She smirked. "Call it a presidential decree."

It wasn't easy to make Sam angry. Even when all his friends were totally ticked off about something, he was usually the one who stayed calm and rational.

But this was too much. What gave Amy Anderson the right to decide what was best for everyone else? She was always shoving her ideas down everyone's throats. Worse than that, she acted like it was her inborn natural right to do it. And to top it off, he was really getting sick of her always putting down his friends. It was time to put a stop to it. *All* of it.

"Fine," he said. His voice came out sounding just as cold as Amy's. "Do what you want, Ms. President. But *I'm* definitely going ahead with the school fair. And you can call *that* whatever you want."

Three

I

An hour later Amy was still fuming.

"I can't believe it," she muttered as she and her friends walked through the chilly afternoon air toward the main entrance to the mall. The thick, puddle gray clouds gathering overhead matched her mood perfectly. "Who does Sam Wells think he is? Everybody loved my idea. How dare he get them all confused with his lame fair?"

Amy shoved the glass revolving door a little harder than necessary. Mel had to hop forward to avoid getting her heels bumped. But Amy hardly noticed. She was too busy trying to figure out what had happened back there at the student council meeting.

She kept coming back to one point— Sam had done it again. He had dared to stand up to The Amys. And he had seemed really serious about his idiotic fair idea. That wasn't so strange—Sam was pretty serious about everything he did. The weird, freaky, totally unbelievable thing was that some of the other student council members had taken it seriously, too. What was *that* all about? Had they totally forgotten who she was? Had they forgotten that she was the student body president? Most important—had they forgotten that she was *Amy Anderson?*

Aimee's big blue eyes were round with sympathy. "I couldn't believe it, either," she said.

Mel shrugged. "Don't worry about it," she advised. "Once the other kids see that we're serious about our fashion show, they'll forget all about Sam Wells and his pathetic little sideshow." She grinned. "After all, we're The Amys. And he's just Sam."

Amy couldn't help smiling back. Somehow Mel always knew the right thing to say to cheer her up. And she was right. There was no sense focusing on the past. The future was the only thing that mattered—wasn't that what Daddy always said?

"Right," she said briskly. Her mind had already moved on. Sam Wells didn't matter. At least not right now. After The Amys ran the greatest fund-raiser Robert Lowell Middle School had ever seen, there would be plenty of time to further humiliate Sam.

But right now they had work to do. That was why they were at the mall.

"Okay, let's be organized about this," Amy went on. She glanced around the wide, palm-lined main aisle of the mall. "We'll work our way down the left side of the aisle first. Let's hit every reasonably cool clothing store and ask them to loan us outfits for the show."

"Sounds good," Mel agreed. "Should we try to borrow different stuff from different places? Or look for the total jackpot from one store?"

Amy shrugged. "We can play that by ear," she said. She smiled, looking forward to seeing the look on Sam's face when she stood up at lunch tomorrow and announced the fashion show to the whole school. "I'll do most of the talking, okay? We'll have everything we need in no time."

II

"I'm sorry," said the droopy-eyed salesclerk at The Gap. "I don't think my manager would go for it." She shrugged. "The last time we did lend our clothes out, everything came back all stretched out and stained with makeup. And that fashion show was run by adults. Some country club, I think."

Amy frowned. This was getting really tiresome. Everyone who worked at this mall seemed to think that all eighth graders were a bunch of irresponsible clothing thieves. Nobody trusted them enough to loan as much as a few measly outfits.

She stomped toward the store's entrance without another word, almost knocking over a table full of pigment-dyed T-shirts on her way. Aimee and Mel were one step behind her as she burst out into the mall's main aisle again.

"Maybe this fashion show isn't such a great idea after all," Aimee said wearily.

"My feet are starting to hurt." She plopped down on a bench in the center of the aisle.

Amy glared at her. "We can't give up," she said. "Come on, Stylistics is just a few stores down. They've got to listen to us." Stylistics was her absolute favorite place to shop for clothes. She spent so much time there that every employee on the staff knew her on sight.

"If they don't want to lend us stuff, you could threaten to stop shopping there," Mel said jokingly, tossing her long, straight black hair back over her shoulder. "They'd be afraid of going out of business."

III

"Can I help y—oh! Hello, Miss Anderson," said the tall, slender manager of Stylistics. She was standing behind the marble counter near the front of the store, watching as one of the clerks counted the money in the register. The manager patted her perfectly coifed auburn hair and gave Amy a polite little smile. "What can we help you with today? We just got in some of those crushed-velvet shirts you were asking about last week."

27

"Hello, Lydia," Amy replied smoothly. The clerk looked up and greeted her politely, but Amy ignored the young girl and directed her gaze at the manager alone. *Go straight to the top.* Daddy's first rule of business. "Actually I'm not here to shop for myself today. I've got a business proposition for you." Quickly she outlined her plans for the fashion show. "Since Stylistics is by far the most fashionable store in the area," she finished, "I'm making you a special offer. I'm willing to let your store be the exclusive supplier of outfits for our show."

"Hmmm." Lydia raised one thin, carefully shaped eyebrow. "Intriguing. But you said it was a business proposition, my dear. What's in it for me?"

Amy hadn't really thought about that. *Business is a two-way street.* That was another saying Daddy liked to toss around. But what was Lydia after?

"There's no money in the budget to pay for the clothes," Aimee whispered.

"No kidding," Amy muttered back, wishing that Aimee would learn to whisper more quietly. Lydia was smirking down at them, her greenish blue eyes looking amused. Mel had taken a step back and was staring down at her own feet.

Amy had no idea what the manager wanted from them. What would her father do in a situation like this?

"I've got an idea," Lydia said after an awkward moment of silence. "You girls can borrow all the clothes you want if you can promise me plenty of free advertising for the store. How about that?"

"That sounds perfect," Amy said quickly. "I was just about to suggest the same thing myself. You've got yourself a deal. We'll be back to pick out the clothes in a few days."

She hurried out of the store before the woman could change her mind, not even pausing to examine the racks of tantalizing clothes all around her. There would be plenty of time to check them out later.

"How are we going to advertise for them?" Mel asked as they stepped out of the store and paused beside the coin-clogged fountain in the middle of the aisle.

"That's easy," Amy replied. Now that

her fashion show plans were really rolling, she felt fantastic. Cool and confident. More than ready for anything Sam Wells and his loser patrol threw her way. "This is where being the editors of the school paper really comes in handy," she explained to her friends with a wicked grin. "Now let's go reward ourselves—by doing some *major* shopping!"

Amy Anderson

How to beat Sam Wells's stupid, idiotic, totally wigged-out idea:

Make sure everyone knows that The Amys are totally, completely, a million percent against it (as if there's any doubt!);

Make sure everyone knows that The Amys think anyone who supports such a lame, babyish idea is a total loser (ditto);

Make sure everyone knows that Stylistics will be supplying the clothes for the show. That will kill two birds with one stone (advertising for the store and letting people know that this will be a serious fashion event);

Start dressing even more fabulously than usual (Aimee and Mel, too) to get everyone psyched for the fashion show.

Just in case the above don't work well enough, <u>figure</u> <u>out</u> <u>ways</u> <u>to</u> <u>sabotage</u> <u>the</u> <u>stupid</u> <u>fair!</u>

Four

"What do you think?" Jordan Sullivan asked.

Sam glanced up from his seat at the foot of Jordan's bed. When he saw what Jordan had drawn, he couldn't help laughing. It was a cartoon featuring a huge, pumped-up superhero type with School Fair written across his chest. The dude was stomping down the street, holding the Robert Lowell school building above his head with his muscular arms. Under the superhero's feet The Amys were running away in terror, dressed in wacky high-fashion outfits, complete with huge stacked heels. But it was clear that the super hero was about to squash them to a pulp. The caption underneath read Sam Strikes Back at Fashion Freaks. The whole thing reminded Sam of one of those political cartoons for adults that Carrie was always clipping out of *The Seattle Times* and hanging on her bedroom door to bug her parents.

"Funny, bro," he told Jordan. "But somehow I don't think that's quite the way to go with our advertising."

"Spoken like a true politician," Sky Foley said with a grin, looking up from the list she was making. She was sprawled on her stomach on Jordan's bedroom floor, her long, curly dark hair sticking out in all directions and a pen tucked behind each ear. "Toss them a compliment before you slam their goofy ideas."

Jordan stuck out his tongue at Sky, and she giggled.

Carrie Mersel leaned over the side of the bed and examined Jordan's drawing. "I have to disagree with you, Sam," she said, running a hand through her dyed black hair. "It kind of works for me. Maybe it will strike fear into The Amys' hearts. If they have hearts, that is—which I suspect they don't. Personally I think they're actually infernal demons, here on earth in human guise to wreak their evil havoc."

"I don't know," Sam said, thinking back to the icy look in Amy's blue eyes. "Demons or not, I don't think The Amys scare too easily."

"That's the understatement of the year," Alex Wagner put in wryly. "Come on, Sam. I wrote down all the events. But we need to figure out how to price everything."

"Gotcha," Sam said, instantly focused again. It was amazing how energetic he felt when he was doing stuff like this. Planning. Making things happen.

He crossed the room and looked over Alex's shoulder. She was sitting at Jordan's desk, making a list of all the games and activities they had planned so far for the fair. Sam read over her list quickly.

Price list:
Dunking booth
Pony rides
Skateboarding exhibition
Brick's band
Jordan's caricature booth
Astrology/fortune-teller (Sky's mom)
Haunted house (Carrie Mersel's Mansion of Menace)
Sideshow games (beanbag toss, dart balloons, etc.)

"Okay," Sam said. "First of all, we have to figure out how much to charge people just to get into the fair. Once they pay the admission price, some of the stuff on this list should be free—like the music and the skateboarding."

"So we're having this thing a week from Saturday, right?" Alex asked, popping her gum.

"That's what Principal Cashen agreed to," Sam answered. Jordan and Carrie laughed quietly, and Sam tried to sneak a peek at their new banner sketch.

"What?" Carrie asked. "You don't trust us?"

"It just has to be serious this time," Sam said. "We have a lot to get·done."

"Sir, yes sir," Jordan joked.

"Politicians have no vision," Carrie complained.

Sam turned back to Alex and Sky. "Next we have to figure out how much people will be willing to pay for that other stuff. We don't want to overcharge, or nobody will have any fun."

"We don't want to *under*charge, either," Alex pointed out. She tucked a stray strand of dark blond hair behind her ear. "Otherwise we won't raise any money. We've got to find—um, what do you call it . . . you know, when you find just the right amount of something. . . ."

"A happy medium," Carrie supplied without looking up from her work. She was carefully filling in some words on Jordan's banner with a red marking pen.

"Right," Sam agreed. "Sky, why don't you try to come up with some fair prices. Then we can all take a look. Alex, how about making up some sign-up sheets to hang up at school tomorrow? We're going to need a lot of help from the other students. Maybe we can hold a big planning meeting on Monday afternoon."

Alex shrugged. "Okay," she said agreeably, reaching for a clean piece of paper. "What are you going to do?"

"I want to make a master list of everything we have to think about," Sam said, grabbing a pencil and a spare sheet of typing paper from Jordan's desk. "You know—food, activities, advertising, tickets, decorations, power supply. . . ."

Sky's dark eyes widened. "Power supply!" she repeated. "Wow. I guess we'll need that so Brick's band will have someplace to plug their instruments in, huh? I never would have thought of that."

"That's why *you're* not student body treasurer, Einstein," Jordan joked.

Sky rolled her eyes. "Thanks a lot, Jor-*dumb*," she replied sarcastically.

Sam wasn't listening to his friends' familiar bickering. His mind was already on his list. He chewed on the end of his pencil and thought. There was so much to keep track of that his mind seemed to be filled to overflowing with details and plans. But with his friends' help he was sure he could make this fund-raiser a success.

It was going to be positively colossal!

Five

By lunchtime on Friday, Amy was getting really sick of seeing posters for Sam's stupid fair. They were plastered everywhere. Of course, they were ugly and tacky—just one of Jordan Sullivan's juvenile cartoons run off on a copier. But that didn't seem to be stopping the other students from looking at them. Why were they bothering? Everyone already knew what was going to happen. The fair would flop in a big way. And the fashion show would be a huge success. It was the way things worked. Still, seeing those ridiculous little posters everywhere was awfully irritating—like being trapped in a car with a mosquito.

Amy headed into the cafeteria, ignoring the posters hung on each of the big double doors. Aimee and Mel were already seated at their usual table.

But Amy's attention was instantly

drawn away from her friends. Her gaze fixed on the round table near the windows where Sam and his little clique of nerds always sat. Right now there was a small crowd gathered around the table. Eddie, Janine, Krysta . . . all the student council reps were there. They were each holding a small stack of multicolored papers.

Amy's eyes narrowed, and her fists clenched involuntarily at her sides. She had a hunch about what was going on here. And she was going to put a stop to it right now.

She stormed over to the table. "What's happening?" she demanded sharply. "Did someone forget to tell me about a student council meeting?" She noticed Carrie smirking at her, but she decided to let it pass this time. Work before pleasure.

Sam's dark eyes were amused as he glanced up at her. "Hi, Amy," he said. "I was just passing out flyers for the school fair. These guys are going to put them in mailboxes around town over the weekend."

Amy put her hands on her hips. "Oh, really?" she spat out. "Since when are the student council reps your personal slaves, *Treasurer* Wells? Besides, I don't think you should call it the *school* fair. That makes it sound like it's the official student council fund-raiser. And it's not. The only official fund-raiser is the one being run by the president and vice president of the student council. And that's the fashion show."

"Don't be mad, Amy," Krysta wheedled, her green eyes wide and innocent looking. "We're just helping out. But don't worry— we'll definitely help you with your fashion show, too. We'll do anything you want."

Amy ignored her. She grabbed one of the flyers to check it out.

"Oh, please." Amy made her voice as haughty and disdainful as she could. "Do you people really think anyone wants to waste their time with this sort of childish stuff?" She tossed the flyer aside. It fluttered to the table in front of Jordan. "Take my advice—give up on this whole idea right now. It's just a big waste of your time." She shrugged and glanced around the table. "Not that you people have much else to do, but still . . ."

Krysta dropped her stack of flyers on

the table and took a step toward Amy. "So what's happening with the fashion show, anyway?" she asked eagerly. "If you need my help right now—or this weekend—I'm totally there! Just say the word."

Amy frowned. The truth was, after her deal with Stylistics the afternoon before, she had hardly thought about the fashion show. After all, they hadn't even set a date for it yet. Why rush things? The school trip wasn't for a couple of months.

Unfortunately that meant she didn't have any orders to pass out to the reps right now. She didn't have any way to distract them from Sam's silly flyers. They were all staring at her expectantly, waiting for her to say something.

Her frown grew deeper. She could feel her cheeks starting to turn pink with rage and frustration. She had to get away and cool down before anyone noticed. "Um, thanks, Krysta," she muttered. "I'll get back to you on that."

She whirled and hurried away.

But not before she saw the satisfied smirk on Sam Wells's face.

<u>Alex Wagner's Book of Deep Thoughts</u>

<u>Entry #15</u>

I was just thinking about how even best friends are always discovering new stuff about each other.

Let me explain. I always thought I knew everything there was to know about Sam. I mean, we've been friends forever, right? But I don't think I've ever seen him as excited about anything as he is about this fair. (Not even skateboarding. Go figure!)

Yesterday (Friday) we hung up the sign-up sheets I made, and by the end of the day they were totally filled. <u>Everybody</u> wants to help with the fair! After our little encounter with Amy at lunchtime I was afraid she was going to stand up and make one of her public announcements—you know, tell everyone to boycott the fair or something. But luckily she didn't. Which just goes to show that maybe The Amys aren't as predictable as I thought. . . .

Anyway, back to my point. After school

Sam came over to my place and we started calling the kids who'd signed up. We told each person that we're definitely having a meeting after school on Monday and asked them to come. Well, after about the first ten names, I was getting totally bored and stir-crazy. I wanted to knock off for a while and do some boarding. Or at least watch a little TV or something.

But not Sam. The more calls he made, the happier he got. It was like he got a rush from the whole thing. He could hardly wait to make some more calls today when we all meet at Sky's place.

It was kind of weird to see him like that. But kind of nice, too. Sam's usually so quiet and thoughtful that sometimes he just kind of fades into the background. Especially next to chatterboxes like Carrie and Jordan. Or Sky. Or even me.

But this political stuff is really bringing out the best in him. It's letting him show off a whole new side of his personality. And I, for one, think that's great.

Six

"The new posters look totally cool, Jordan!" Sam exclaimed.

Carrie snorted. "Could you repeat that, Sam?" she said. "I don't think he heard you the first eleven dozen times you said it."

Sam grinned at her and bit into his sandwich. It was lunchtime on Monday. And everything was going great. Awesome, in fact.

He had hardly thought about anything but the fair all weekend. He'd planned. Made lists. Drawn charts. Called vendors. It was amazing how fast it was all coming together—thanks to all the help his friends had given him. And after the big meeting with the other volunteers later this afternoon, it could only get better.

This was going to be the best fundraiser Robert Lowell had ever seen!

Sky swallowed a bite of her bean-sprout-and-lentil-stuffed pita sandwich. "I have to agree with Sam, no matter how many times he repeats himself," she said. "The posters look pretty awesome. Maybe Jor-dumb isn't totally useless after all."

"Thanks a bunch, granola brain." Jordan stuck out his tongue at her, then broke into a pleased grin. "Still, I can't take all the credit for this one. My immense, awe-inspiring talent is only partly responsible. Sam's buddies in the nerd lab added the special effects."

Sam's gaze wandered to another table a few yards away, and he watched as a short, skinny guy with glasses used his spoon to shoot a spoonful of mashed potatoes at a chubby boy with braces and a bowl haircut. A tall, very pale-skinned girl who was sitting with them laughed so hard that milk started to come out of her nose.

Sam smiled and turned away. His friends liked to give him a hard time about hanging out in the school computer lab during his free study period. And it was true that most of the kids he'd befriended there—Dwight Durham, Al Isakoff, Becky Yarborough, and the others—weren't exactly popularity junkies. But Sam thought they were interesting. And they definitely knew what they were doing with a mouse and a modem.

"Dwight does good work." Sam shifted his gaze to one of the posters in question.

It was hanging on the wall near the lunch line, where nobody could miss it when they entered the cafeteria. Hand-drawn rainbow neon letters six inches high shouted Be at the Fair or Be Square! Beneath that was a photo of the school. Dwight had scanned it into the computer, then used a computer design program to add fireworks, confetti, and musical notes spewing out of it. He had also managed to make the building look like it was dancing by squiggling the photo so the outlines were wavy. The date, time, and ticket price were listed at the bottom of the poster.

The posters looked totally professional. They were also pretty eye-catching.

Carrie snorted again. "Computer-enhanced posters," she muttered. "What will we have next? Robotic pets instead of cats and dogs? Silicon chips in our sandwiches to help us digest?"

Carrie hated computers with a passion matched only by her disdain for The Amys. But Sam could tell that she wasn't really upset about this. She was just kidding around—being Carrie. Maybe she wasn't nuts about the posters, but she was totally behind the fair. She had even voluntarily started a discussion with her mother to talk about the pony rides.

The others were really coming through, too. Jordan had spent his entire Saturday afternoon working on the posters with Dwight. Alex had helped out a lot with all the phone calls they had to make, plus she was organizing the fair's skateboard rally. And on Sunday afternoon Sky had done what she did best—dragged them all to the mall. But this time she'd had a more important purpose than ferreting out the best price on purple nail polish. She'd led the way in asking the stores to let them hang up posters for the fair.

Planning this fair together was bringing out the best in all of them, Sam decided contentedly. That was the great thing about a project like this. Everyone working as a team, helping out, cooperating. He couldn't wait for the meeting after school that day. Then they could really get rolling. . . .

"Hey, everyone, listen up!" a familiar voice shouted at that moment, interrupting Sam's thoughts.

He looked up quickly. Sure enough, it was Amy. With all the excitement of planning the fair, he'd almost forgotten about her.

She was standing on a chair at The Amys' regular lunch table. As usual everyone in the cafeteria had fallen silent immediately at the sound of her voice. Now they were all gazing at her expectantly.

"Uh-oh," Carrie muttered. "What's the wicked witch of the Northwest up to now?"

Sam gulped. He didn't even want to know the answer to that. Amy was basking in her audience's attention as if she'd just been crowned queen of the universe. How did she manage to look so smug and self-confident all the time? And why did everyone always fall for it?

"Thanks so much for your attention," Amy purred, running one hand casually through her smooth blond hair. "Speaking as your student body president, I have an important announcement to make. I think you're all going to be really excited about it." For the briefest moment her gaze rested on Sam's face, and the edges of her lips curled up in a slight smile.

"Maybe she's moving to Siberia," Jordan whispered. "I'd be pretty excited about that."

Sam didn't even crack a grin at the joke. He felt as if an icy cold hand had just squeezed his heart. He recognized the look in Amy's cool blue eyes. It was the look that meant she was about to do something mean. Something devious. Something to get him back for shooting down her idea.

"I'm sure I don't have to tell you how glamorous modeling is," Amy went on, addressing the room at large as casually as if she were chatting with her best friends. "The cool fashions, the hip people, the jet-set lifestyle." She paused again and smiled. "Well, very soon some of you in this very room will have a chance to be models yourselves. In our school fund-raising fashion show!"

A murmur of excitement went up from the crowd. At tables all around him Sam saw people whispering to each other and leaning forward in their seats to hear what Amy would say next.

Alex shook her head, her forehead creasing into a worried frown. "What's she up to now?" she murmured.

"Trouble," Carrie replied darkly. "The same thing she's always up to."

Amy paused long enough this time to let the excitement really build. Seated behind her at the table, Aimee and Mel were smiling triumphantly. Sam drummed his fingers on the table nervously. He had the sinking feeling that this wasn't the end of the announcement. No doubt about it— The Amys were up to something. Something more than simply forging ahead with their fashion show. But what?

He didn't have to wait long for the answer.

"I really hope you'll all come to our modeling tryouts," Amy said. "We'll be holding them today. Right after school."

Amy Anderson
<u>Notes</u> <u>to</u> <u>Myself</u>

Always remember Daddy's second rule of business: <u>Timing</u> <u>is</u> everything!

The Many Moods of Sam Wells

MONDAY: LUNCHTIME. Sam is flabbergasted by Amy's announcement. He can't believe she would hold her modeling tryouts at the same time as his big meeting. Of course everyone will choose Amy over him. The meeting is ruined! The fair is ruined! This is a disaster!

MONDAY: 1:57 P.M. Sam passes a group of kids talking in the hall in front of one of his posters. When they see him, they all stop talking and just stare at him. As he walks away he hears them start to giggle and whisper. He is sure he's never been so humiliated in his entire life.

MONDAY: 2:15 P.M. Sam feels completely discouraged. But Carrie gives him an impassioned lecture about how important it is not to let The Amys win. She even throws in some stirring words about the American Revolution and the Declaration of Independence. Sam decides she's right. He can't just give up on the fair now. They've all worked too hard to give up without a fight. He'll go ahead with the meeting that afternoon. If nobody shows up, *then* he can give up.

MONDAY: 3:00 P.M. Sam is nervous. On his way to his meeting he stops by the computer lab to pick up the disk with Jordan's poster on it. A couple of his computer buddies are there, including Dwight Durham. Dwight tells Sam he thinks the fair is the first school event he's ever been excited about. That reminds Sam of his responsibilities to the entire student body. He has to do what's best for them.

MONDAY: 3:06 P.M. Sam arrives in the auditorium and sees that about a dozen kids have showed up. It's not nearly as many as he'd hoped for before Amy's announcement. But it's better than he hoped for *after* Amy's announcement. So things could be worse. Feeling a mixture of disappointment and relief, he starts the meeting.

MONDAY: 4:19 P.M. Sam is feeling much happier. People have been trickling in and out of his meeting. *Lots* of people. Most of them are really excited about auditioning for Amy's fashion show. But they want to help with the fair, too, so they are stopping in at Sam's meeting before or after they try out for Amy. And thanks to all the organizing he did over the weekend, Sam manages to get a lot accomplished even with all the comings and goings. Okay, so maybe the fashion show is still the talk of the school. Maybe it's certain to be a huge success. But it seems that his fair is going to be a success, too—no matter what The Amys think of it!

MONDAY: 4:35 P.M. The football coach stops by the meeting to donate some extra rolls of tickets to use for the fair. Sam is jubilant. Now they can sell tickets in advance instead of just at the door! That will guarantee that a lot of people will come. If they've already paid for a ticket, they're less likely to forget. Everything is working out just great!

MONDAY: 9:45 P.M. Sam is still feeling happy about the way things are going. His friends are pumped. The other volunteers are raring to go. Everyone has promised to sell tickets to their families and friends. Sam is even starting to feel a little bit sorry for Amy. Sure, she held her auditions. But she hasn't even bothered to advertise or sell tickets to her show. He realizes he doesn't even know when it is. He hopes she won't be *too* hurt and humiliated if no one shows up.

TUESDAY: JUST BEFORE HOMEROOM. Walking into school, Sam notices something strange. The posters advertising the fair are gone. All of them. They've been replaced by huge, gaudy posters . . . advertising the fashion show! They don't have much information. Just a glossy photo of The Amys dressed in stylish outfits. And the words *Coming Soon!* Sam doesn't remember the last time he was so angry.

TUESDAY: A FEW SECONDS LATER. A pale and angry Alex finds Sam at his locker and gives him the bad news. She just overheard a couple of seventh-grade girls gossiping. There's going to be an official announcement today at lunch. But everyone is already talking about it.

The Amys are holding their fashion show on Saturday—at the exact same time as Sam's fair!

Now Sam is mad. *Really* mad. This is war!

Seven

Amy loved this feeling. The one she always got when she totally triumphed.

"Did you see the look on his face when I made the announcement today?" she gloated as she walked down the hall with her friends after school on Tuesday.

Aimee's eyes gleamed. "Definitely," she said. "It was better than TV. This should teach him not to mess with us."

"This almost feels too easy," Mel commented. "Do you think he'll do something to get back at us? You know— try to mess up the fashion show or whatever?"

Amy grinned. "That's the best part," she crowed. "You know how Sam is. Totally honest. Totally responsible. He didn't even tattle to Principal Cashen about the posters." She was particularly proud of that. It hadn't been easy to get all those fancy posters made up overnight. It hadn't been cheap, either—but she'd figure out a story to take care of that before her mother's credit card bill came.

In any case, it had definitely been worth it. She and her friends had come to school a half hour early that morning to make the switch. Then they had left again and made a fashionably late entrance right before homeroom. That way it looked as if the posters had just appeared overnight, like magic. It gave things just the right touch of drama. Kept the Amy mystique thriving.

"Good point," Mel said as the three girls paused beside Aimee's locker. "Sam does have a pretty bad case of goody-goody syndrome." She grinned. "Hey, maybe we should start calling him Mr. Fair. Get it?"

Aimee glanced up from rummaging through her locker. She looked slightly puzzled.

But Amy laughed. "Good one, Mel," she said approvingly. When it came to people like Sam Wells, Mel could be just a tiny bit too softhearted and nice sometimes. Amy was glad to see that this wasn't one of those times. "Anyway, I don't think we have to worry," she went on, leaning against the red metal doors of the nearby lockers. "There's nothing Sam could do to us even if he wanted to. But if he tries anything, we'll be ready."

"Yeah, and if we have to, we can send out our attack models," Mel joked.

Right, the models. Maybe the audition hadn't broken up Sam's silly meeting as Amy had hoped. But it had hardly been a complete waste of time, either. Amy never would have guessed that they could actually find fifteen tolerable models in the generally uncool population of Robert Lowell Middle School. But they had managed. That called for a celebration in itself.

"Come on," she suggested as Aimee finally finished rooting through her locker and slammed it shut. "Let's go to Stylistics and decide which outfits we want everyone to wear."

Aimee looked surprised. "I thought we were going to sell tickets today."

Amy shrugged. "We've got plenty of time for that," she said casually. "If we wait long enough, people will be knocking down our doors to get them."

Knock, knock!

Amy rapped the door knocker sharply a few more times. Then she stepped back and waited, tapping her foot impatiently.

"I'm freezing," Mel grumbled, wrapping her arms more tightly around herself.

"Next time wear a jacket," Amy snapped irritably.

She wasn't about to admit it, but she was cold, too. Not to mention tired. It was already getting dark out, and a damp, chilly breeze was blowing in off Puget Sound and cutting straight through her stylish cabled tights, turning her legs to ice. The last place in the world she felt like being was this pathetic neighborhood in the lower-middle-class section of Taylor Haven, where the biggest house on the block was smaller than the Andersons' three-car garage.

But none of those things was the main reason that Amy was feeling crankier with each passing second. The main reason was that she and her friends had been going door-to-door since they'd left the mall an hour ago. And so far they'd only sold two measly tickets to the fashion show.

"What's wrong with people?" Amy muttered under her breath, hopping from foot to foot to keep warm. She was just reaching for the knocker again when the door finally swung open.

"Can I help you?" asked the breathless, moon-faced young woman who stood in the doorway.

Amy felt like wrinkling her nose as she glanced past the woman into a living room decorated in a style that could only be described as early psychotic toddler. Stuffed animals and brightly colored plastic toys were scattered everywhere. The only good thing about that was they almost covered the cheap, tacky furniture.

Amy forced herself to smile at the woman. "Hello," she said. "My name is Amy Anderson. My friends and I are selling tickets to our school fashion show fundraiser. It's this Saturday, and it's guaranteed to be the most stylish event of the season. Would you and your family like to come?"

From somewhere beyond the living room a baby started to wail. The woman glanced over her shoulder worriedly. "Oh, I'm sorry," she said, sounding distracted. "I'm afraid we're busy on Saturday."

Amy let out a sigh of frustration. That was exactly what almost everyone else had told them, too! Since when did the people around here have such busy social calendars?

She couldn't take it anymore. "What could you possibly be doing that's more exciting than our fashion show?" she demanded.

The woman looked surprised at her outburst. But she answered politely, only glancing over her shoulder once or twice in the direction of the crying baby. "Actually if you'd asked me a few hours ago, we wouldn't have been doing anything," she said. "But some other kids stopped by just now and sold me tickets to a fair up at the middle school. That's on Saturday, too. I'm afraid we can't do both."

The woman said good-bye and shut the door.

Amy's fists were clenched tightly at her sides. She whirled around to face her friends, hardly noticing the cold anymore. They both looked just as angry as she felt.

"Sam!" they all cried in unison.

Eight

"Show me the number again," Jordan begged playfully, clasping his hands in front of him. "Please! Just one more time!"

Alex grinned and shoved her notebook across the lunch table toward him. "Read it and weep," she declared. "These advance tickets were an awesome idea! We made more selling them door-to-door yesterday than we thought we'd take in from the whole fair."

Sam nodded. He didn't blame Jordan for wanting to see the numbers again. He leaned over Alex's shoulder to take another look himself. It was pretty unbelievable. "The Amys will never beat this," he murmured.

Carrie heard him. "No way," she agreed contentedly, reaching across the table to snag a handful of Jordan's potato chips. "Now that Sam Wells, Supertreasurer, is on the scene, all The Amys can do is slink back to their putrid den, lick their wounds, and admit the truth. They're a bunch of total political losers."

Sky looked up and laughed. "Putrid den?" she repeated. "Where do you come up with this stuff, Carrie? And when are you going to become an official ghostwriter for Stephen King?"

"Hey! Take that back, Foley," Carrie said. "King is the king, and he does not have other people write for him."

"Speaking of writers . . . ," said a new voice from behind Sam. A voice that sounded a little too pleased with itself.

Sam spun around in his seat. Amy was standing there with her hands behind her back—and a very smug expression on her face.

"What do you want?" Carrie demanded. "If you're looking for help adding up your ticket sales, just remember—anything multiplied by zero equals zero."

Amy didn't even acknowledge Carrie's remark. She was staring at Sam. Once again her eyes held that scary, sneaky look. "The latest issue of the paper just came out," she said casually. "Hot off the presses. I thought you guys should be the first ones to see it."

She pulled something out from behind her back and tossed it on the table. It was a copy of the *Robert Lowell Observer*, the school's weekly newspaper.

"This can't be good," Sky whispered under her breath.

Sam's eyes were already riveted on the front-page headline:

FASHION FEVER SWEEPS SCHOOL!

"You can keep this copy," Amy said sweetly. "I'm sure you'll want to read every word." She spun on her heel and swept away toward her own table.

Sam hardly noticed. He was too busy scanning the article under the headline.

"What does it say?" Alex asked, craning her neck to try to read it. "Read it out loud."

"Do I have to?" Sam muttered.

Carrie grabbed the paper out of his hands. "I'll read it," she said. She cleared her throat. "'Fashion Freaks'—uh, I mean

'Fashion Fever Sweeps School, by Mel Eng.'" She paused and grimaced. "Whose warped idea was it to let those three airheads run the paper, anyway?"

"Read the article," Sky begged. "The suspense is killing me."

Carrie nodded and started to read. "'Paris, Milan, New York . . . and now Ocean's View, Washington. These are the fashion capitals of the world.'" She paused again and snorted derisively. "Oh, give me a break!"

This time Alex snatched the paper. "Here, let me do it," she said. "We don't have time for Carrie's comments." She looked down at the story. "Okay, Paris, Milan, blah blah blah . . . 'This Saturday, for one day only, the glamorous and exciting world of cutting edge fashion—"

"Like anything in Ocean's Edge could ever be *cutting* edge," Carrie interjected.

"Excuse me. I'm trying to read here," Alex scolded. She cleared her throat. "'The exciting world of haute couture will be taking over the Robert Lowell Middle School auditorium. The event is open to the public on a first-come, first-served basis, and tickets will be sold at the door. Clothing is being provided by Stylistics, the popular local boutique, and the models are an elite group of students chosen from an extremely competitive field of applicants. Best of all, every cent of the money raised by this once-in-a-lifetime event will be used for this year's school trip. If the turnout is as outstanding as the event's organizers are expecting, the entire middle school could soon have enough money in their budget to go just about anywhere! How about Paris?'" Alex finished reading and looked up. "Ugh! What a stupid article!"

"Tell me about it," Carrie declared. "What makes The Amys think people will really fall for that kind of garbage?"

Sam pointed to a large ad just below the article. "Check this out," he said grimly. "They're even advertising for the store that's giving them the clothes."

Suddenly Sky let out a squeal. "Eww!" she cried. She was staring at the article just beneath the Stylistics ad. "Check *that* out!"

Sam followed her gaze. He gulped. "Uh-oh," he muttered.

BY AMY ANDERSON

My fellow students, in the past few days many of you may have seen some flashy posters advertising a fair this weekend. Some of you may even be considering attending this so-called fund-raiser. However, this reporter—you probably know me best as your unanimously elected student body president—has discovered some disturbing information about this fair, which I felt it was my duty to pass along. I think you should all consider this information carefully before making any plans.

The fair is a fraud. The organizers do not represent the entire school. They are a small group of students with tastes that are, shall we say, a bit out of the mainstream. Do you really want to spend your Saturday listening to an obscure heavy metal rock band? Talking with aging hippies about the moon and stars? "Enjoying" hokey entertainment planned by people who have trouble planning their own wardrobes?

I didn't think so. That's why I would like to humbly suggest an alternative. A cool, exciting, and very entertaining fund-raiser, fully supported by your student body president and vice president. A fabulous, fun, and fantastic fashion show! For more information on this important event, please see the article above.

See you on the catwalk!

Sam looked up and met his friends' eyes one by one. Alex looked stunned. Jordan looked worried. Sky seemed to be on the verge of tears. And Carrie was obviously ready to kill someone—namely Amy.

"It's really more of an editorial than an article, don't you think?" Sam commented ruefully. He rubbed his forehead and glanced down at the headline again. "Wow. Talk about bad press."

"Guys? Why don't we just go to Principal Cashen? Maybe he can work it out so that our fund-raisers aren't competing," Sky suggested.

"No way," Carrie said. "We're not going to run whining to an adult. The Amys would have a field day with that."

"Besides, all Cashen would do is tell us to find a mature way to work things out on our own," Jordan put in. "That's all our wuss principal ever says."

Carrie slammed her milk carton down on the table so hard, she caused white droplets to spatter out. "We can't let them get away with this," she fumed, her hazel eyes shooting fire. She paged through the rest of the newspaper, turning the pages so forcefully that a couple of them ripped. "Look! They didn't even print our column, Jordan!"

Jordan shrugged. "Big surprise there," he said.

Sam sighed. Carrie and Jordan wrote a weekly column for the *Observer.* This week it had been all about the fair. Carrie had described the activities and events in detail, and Jordan had drawn several fun and witty cartoons to go along with it. The column had made the fair sound like a total blast. It was a shame—that kind of advertising really could have put them over the top.

Carrie flipped back to the front page again and jabbed her finger at Amy's article. "I can't believe her nerve," she hissed. "How could she put this piece of total trash on the front page and call it news?"

"It really stinks," Sky put in timidly. She shrugged. "Although it's kind of funny in a way, since if you think about it, your column was pretty opinionated, too. . . ." Her voice trailed off and she gulped.

Sam winced. He knew Carrie wasn't going to let Sky get away with that. Even if they all knew she hadn't meant anything bad by it.

Carrie whirled around in her seat and glared at Sky, who already looked very sorry she'd opened her mouth. "What are you talking about?" she yelled. "A weekly column isn't the same thing as a front-page news story! She's trying to trick everyone into thinking she's reporting facts here." She jabbed at the page again. "Don't tell me she's tricked you, too? I didn't think you were *that* gullible, Sky!"

"That's not what I meant," Sky protested feebly. "I—I—"

Alex jumped in and rescued her. "Forget it, you two," she said sharply. "This is no time for us to start arguing with each other. We've got to come up with a plan. A way to fight back against The Amys. Some kind of, um . . . what do you call it? It starts with an *r*, I think. . . . Not *revenge*. . . ."

"*Retaliation*," Carrie said immediately. "And you're right, Alex."

Sky nodded and shot Alex a grateful look. "Definitely."

Sam let out a silent sigh of relief. The last thing they needed right now was one of Carrie's famous "freak-outs," as Sky liked to call them. Still, he wasn't sure it made sense to try to retaliate. Maybe they should just move their fair to another day. But at this point all the vendors and workers were set for Saturday. Today was Wednesday. There was nothing they could do.

As if reading Sam's mind, Jordan spoke up. "But what can we do?" he asked, shoving his messy blond bangs out of his eyes. "The damage is done. We could make up more posters, but it will cost money. And they'd probably just rip them down again."

Sam nodded. He had just remembered something. "Besides, think about it," he said. "How many tickets did we sell yesterday? Dozens, right?"

"At least," Alex confirmed.

"So even if nobody else comes and we don't sell any tickets at the door, we're still going to do pretty well," Sam went on. He smiled weakly, trying not to look at the newspaper in front of him. "I mean, it's not like people are going to return tickets they already bought, right?"

76

Skyler Foley's
Anti-Amy Argument

Okay, here are just a few of my least favorite things about The Amys (especially Amy Anderson!):

1. Their attitude: It stinks. They think they own the whole school and that nobody else's opinion counts for anything.

2. Their tactics: That's a word Carrie started using a lot after Amy showed us the newspaper at lunch today. Believe me, that word definitely fits The Amys. They'll do anything to get their way. Even if it's totally mean and unfair and rotten and underhanded and devious, like slamming us in the Observer.

3. Everything else about them: Especially the way they're messing with poor Sam. He's just trying to do what's

right for everybody. And they're trying to ruin it all out of spite. How petty is that?

Okay, I know my parents probably wouldn't approve of this list. They think the world would be a lot more peaceful if everybody just loved everybody else all the time. And they're probably right.

But <u>they</u> don't have to go to school with the evil Amys!

Nine

"Hey there, Amy," Brick, the driver of bus number four, said in his gravelly voice as Amy climbed the steps on Thursday morning.

Amy gave him a quick, dismissive little wave—after all, he was on the side of the enemy—then slid into the front seat. Mel and Aimee were already lounging in the seat right behind hers. "Hi, guys," she greeted them, ignoring the driver, who was humming along with the heavy metal song on the bus radio. "Any news from the geek patrol?"

Mel shot a quick glance toward the backseat of the bus, where Sam and his friends always sat. "They've been pretty quiet so far," she reported.

"Good." Amy smiled as the bus rumbled down the hill toward the turnoff onto Whidbey Road. "Maybe they've finally learned their lesson about messing with us."

"Everyone in school was talking about your article yesterday afternoon," Aimee said, leaning forward and resting her arms on the back of Amy's seat. "They all sounded totally psyched about the fashion show. And totally down on Sam's festival of nerds."

Amy grinned. "I know," she said. "And I don't think anyone even noticed that we 'accidentally' forgot to run the dorky duo's column this week." She corrected herself quickly. "Well, except for Principal Cashen, that is. He was pretty ticked off about it. But I just told him I was soooo sorry, and we'd print an apology in next week's paper."

Mel looked surprised. "Are we really going to apologize?"

"We'll see," Amy replied, flashing a wicked grin. "Next week is ages away. We just might happen to forget all about it by then." She shrugged. "But even if he forces us, who cares? By then our fashion show will already be part of history."

Aimee smirked. "And Sam's lame fair

will be totally forgotten. If it's not already."

The bus wheezed to a stop in front of a big, white, modern house. Carrie Mersel was standing at the end of the driveway. She climbed onto the bus, her black combat boots clomping loudly on each step, and greeted Brick. Then she paused in the aisle next to Amy's seat.

"What are you looking so smug about?" she demanded, glaring at Amy and her friends.

Amy smiled sweetly. "I think that hideous black hair dye you use must be dripping into your eyes and affecting your vision," she cooed. She knew that Carrie was sensitive about her hair. And it was such an easy target. Just like Carrie herself, with her gloomy clothes and her paranoid attitude. "We're just happy," Amy went on. "We're looking forward to Saturday."

"Yeah, I bet," Carrie spat out. "Well, don't look so happy just yet. A lot can happen between now and then." Then she stomped off toward the back of the bus.

Aimee rolled her eyes. "What a freak," she muttered.

"Who cares about her?" Amy said

breezily. "She's just wigged out because she knows nobody is going to come to her silly little fair. They'll all be at our fashion show. Speaking of which, her hair horror reminded me of something. We haven't talked much yet about how we're going to do the models' hair. . . ."

The three friends discussed hair and makeup ideas for the next few minutes. Before Amy knew it, the bus slowed to take the turn into the school driveway.

Mel peered out the window as Brick steered to the curb. "Check it out," she said. "I wonder why all those kids are hanging around outside?"

Amy turned and saw a dozen or so students milling around on the front walk. That *was* a little strange, especially since a light, misty rain was starting to fall. "There's only one way to find out," she said. "Maybe they want to ask us about the fashion show."

The Amys led the way off the bus. Amy glanced around, then grabbed the nearest student, a dark-haired girl named Tiffany Schwartz in a droopy floral-print dress. "Hey, what's going on out here?" Amy asked.

Tiffany seemed surprised that Amy was talking to her. That happened a lot when Amy decided to speak to the little people. She waited patiently for Tiffany to get over her awe and answer the question.

"Oh, uh, hi, Amy," Tiffany said. "I'm just waiting for Sam Wells. I want to talk to him about getting my money back on these stupid fair tickets." She pulled a handful of brightly colored tickets out of her dress pocket and waved them in the air dramatically. "My mom bought them the other day for my whole family, but after I read that article in the paper yesterday, I convinced her we should go to your fashion show instead. My next-door neighbors, too."

Amy exchanged a smile with Aimee and Mel. Then she turned to include Tiffany. "I'm so glad that my article was helpful," she said smoothly. "I just thought everyone should know the truth before they decided which fund-raiser to go to."

Tiffany nodded, looking distracted. Sam had just stepped off the bus. Instantly he was surrounded by kids clamoring for their money back.

Amy paused just long enough to catch his eye. She gave him a long, slow smile of triumph, savoring the shocked and dismayed look on his face.

Then she turned and followed her friends inside.

"Well, at least not that many guys returned their tickets," Alex said hopefully.

"Yeah. We're just lucky The Amys were moronic enough to choose a fund-raiser no self-respecting dude would ever show up for," Jordan added with a slight smile.

"But I can't believe so many people actually fell for their disgusting lies!" Carrie cried.

Sam shook his head wearily. It had to be at least the five-hundredth time she'd said those words, or some more colorful version of them, since school had let out. And that was only half an hour ago. Besides, Sam had been asking himself the same thing over and over again all day, ever since the moment that morning when he'd climbed off the bus and been surrounded by unhappy ticket holders demanding a refund.

"I don't know why you're so surprised," Jordan said glumly. "You know how things work at our school. Everyone listens to everything The Amys say. They believe it, too. Just like a herd of stupid sheep or something."

Sam picked at the thick carpeting on Carrie's bedroom floor. He was leaning against her bed with her phone on his knees.

"Quiet down for a second, okay?" he said. "I want to call a few more vendors."

Sky nodded and smiled tentatively. "At least that's one good thing," she offered. "None of the ones you've called so far have backed out."

Sam just nodded and dialed. He knew that Sky meant well. But her words weren't a whole lot of comfort right now. Maybe their vendors would still be there on Saturday. Maybe they would have plenty of food and games and prizes. But what good would that do if nobody showed up to enjoy it?

Sam had known that The Amys' newspaper nastiness was bad news. He just hadn't realized exactly *how* bad.

*   *   *

"Okay, that's the last one," Sam announced half an hour later. He hung up the phone and stood up to stretch out his back. "All our vendors are still on."

"So what do we do now?" Alex asked, leaning back against the wall in Carrie's rickety old desk chair. "We have to figure out a way to get everyone to change their minds again and come to the fair."

Sam nodded thoughtfully. The Amys had changed everyone's minds once. Maybe he and his friends could find a way to change them back. "Well, we've already got plenty of cool games and booths and stuff lined up. So what else can we do to make people really excited about coming to the fair?"

"We could phone in a bomb threat to the fashion show," Carrie suggested with a wicked glint in her eyes. "I know people worship The Amys, but I bet they're not willing to *die* for them!"

Sam gave her an annoyed look. "Quit goofing around, Carrie," he said. "We need some serious ideas."

"What makes you think I'm not serious?" Carrie countered.

Alex looked worried. "Um, isn't faking bomb threats sort of against the law or something?"

"I'm sure it is," Sam said firmly. "But even if it weren't, we still wouldn't do it. Or anything like it. That kind of thing's just not cool. We're not going to lower ourselves to The Amys' level. I'm an elected school officer now, and I've got responsibilities. I've got to act in the best interest of the school—you know, set an example or whatever. We've got to play by the rules."

He glanced around and saw that the others were all staring at him in astonishment. He felt his face turning red. Okay, so maybe he wasn't usually the kind of guy to burst into impassioned speeches at the drop of a hat. But he meant every word he'd said. Playing tricks and sparring with The Amys was all right in some situations. Maybe. But this was too important.

Sky was the first to break the silence that followed. "Maybe we could lower our ticket prices and offer cool prizes for the sideshow games," she suggested quietly.

Sam smiled at her gratefully. "That's a good idea, Sky," he said. "We could definitely cut prices a little and still make a decent amount of money." He shook his head reluctantly. "The prize thing is a great idea, too. But I think that one's a no-go. We just don't have the bucks to buy anything decent."

"Maybe not," Jordan piped in. "But we could go around to all the stores in town again. Some of the ones that let us hang up our posters might also be willing to donate stuff for prizes. Especially if they know it's for a good cause."

"Awesome idea, man!" Sam exclaimed, smacking himself on the forehead. "Why didn't I think of that? Hey, come to think of it, Dwight Durham's parents own that big pet store at the mall. I bet they'd donate some goldfish or something."

Alex was nodding enthusiastically. "I could call the owner of the Skateboard Shack," she offered. "He's really cool. I'm sure he'd kick in some stuff. Maybe even a board or two!"

Sam grabbed a notebook and a ballpoint pen from Carrie's desk and started scribbling notes. "Great," he said eagerly. "Anybody else have anything?"

The others threw out more ideas. Soon the list of possible prizes filled a whole page of the notebook.

"Now we're getting somewhere." Sam ripped the page with the list on it out of the notebook. "Let's head right out and see if we can bag some of these prizes before dinnertime." He smiled at his friends. "See? This might work out after all. All it takes is a few new ideas and a little teamwork. And I think it's pretty cool that we're taking the high road—you know, that we're not even thinking of doing anything sneaky to ruin The Amys' stupid fashion show, even if they do totally deserve it."

"Right," Carrie said. She exchanged an unreadable glance with Jordan. "We're not thinking about that at all."

Carrie was smiling in a way that made Sam feel just a tiny bit nervous. But he decided not to think about that right now. There was too much work to do.

Sam Wells's
Political Diary

Dateline: Last Chance

Well, I guess we're doing everything we can to make this thing fly. We actually managed to scrounge up a whole pile of awesome prizes this afternoon. Most of the store owners we talked to were really cool about it. And Carrie offered to write up some kind of press-release-type thing to pass out tomorrow in the cafeteria. But just to make sure people get the message, I'm planning to ask Principal Cashen to let me make an announcement during homeroom, too.

I'm really trying to psych up the others and make them think this can work. That a few prizes and a bargain price will convince people to give our fair a shot. To at least stop by for a while on their way to the fashion show. I guess I'm trying to psych myself up, too.

Because pep talks aside, if this stuff doesn't work, I'm all out of ideas. The fair will flop, and that will be that. The Amys will win.

And if I can't even run one lousy little school fair successfully, what makes me think I could ever be a real politician someday?

Ten

I

"May I have your attention, please?" Principal Cashen's voice crackled through the speaker in Amy's homeroom. "We have a special announcement this morning."

Amy glanced up. "Maybe the police are shutting down the cafeteria," she joked. "They finally realized we're all being slowly poisoned by their heinous food."

She was in a good mood. She and Aimee and Mel had spent the previous evening finalizing their plans for Saturday's fashion show. It was going to be incredible. The kind of thing the whole school would be talking about for months. Maybe years.

Aimee giggled and started to respond. But Principal Cashen's voice drowned her out. "So please listen up as I hand over the microphone to your very own school treasurer, Sam Wells."

"Sam?" Mel hissed, sitting up straight in her seat. "What's going on?"

Amy quickly put a finger to her lips. She wanted to hear this. What was Sam up to now? Didn't he even know enough to lie down when he was beaten?

"Thanks, Principal Cashen," Sam's voice came through the PA system. "Greetings, students of Robert Lowell. I'll make this brief. As you probably know, I'm organizing a fund-raising fair tomorrow on the football field. It's sure to be a total blast, and I hope you'll all come by. To make things even better, we're cutting our ticket prices in half—that's half price, people!—and offering chances to win a bunch of cool prizes donated by local businesses. You could win a free CD-ROM game for your computer, a MusicMall gift certificate, a glow-in-the-dark T-shirt, all kinds of cool stuff. We'll even be raffling off a brand-new skateboard!"

Sam signed off a moment later, and Amy let out a snort. "Totally pathetic," she declared. "Is that really the best he can do? Glow-in-the-dark T-shirts?"

Mel cast her an anxious glance. "I don't know," she whispered. "Some of those other prizes sound pretty good. What if people change their minds about coming to our show?"

"What are you, nuts?" Amy retorted.

"No, she's right, Amy," Aimee put in. She sounded kind of worried, too. "You know how stupid and shallow some people are at this school. Who knows? Some of them might be willing to skip something important like our fashion show if they think they can win lots of free junk."

Amy raised one eyebrow and stared at her friends. What were they thinking? If anything, Sam's little announcement should make them all feel more confident than ever. A few measly prizes were nothing next to the power of The Amys. And if this was Sam's best attempt at fighting back, the battle and the war were already won.

Still, she didn't want to blow things by getting too cocky. Maybe Aimee had a point. Maybe some kids *were* stupid enough to fall for Sam's pathetic bribes.

"I guess I could make my own little announcement at lunch today," she mused. "Just to make absolutely sure that nobody is at all confused about what the *real* can't-miss event of the year is."

II

"*Psst!* Carrie," a voice muttered. "Is it ready?"

Carrie turned and saw Jordan standing behind her, glancing nervously from side to side. She slammed her locker door shut. "It's ready," she confirmed gleefully in a low tone.

She scanned the crowded hall to check if any of their other friends were anywhere in sight. It was vital to make sure Sam didn't catch them talking about their current project, code name: Operation Fashion Fry. And she and Jordan had agreed to keep it a secret from the others as well. Alex might not feel right about going behind Sam's back like this, even if it was for his own good. After all, she and Sam had always been pretty close, even within their little group. As for Sky, well, she meant well. But keeping secrets wasn't exactly a strong point with her. She'd be better off not knowing, too.

Jordan rubbed his hands together eagerly. "Cool," he whispered. "Hand it over. I've got study hall before lunch, so I can go down to the computer lab and—"

"Shhh!" Carrie hissed suddenly. She had just spotted three familiar heads bobbing along through the crowd nearby. Two blond heads and one dark. "Amy alert."

Jordan nodded. Without another word he opened his math book. Carrie pulled a sheet of paper out of her English folder, and quickly slipped it into Jordan's textbook.

Jordan slammed the book shut and nodded briskly. Then he hurried away down the hall.

Carrie grinned as Jordan disappeared around the corner. Then she turned and watched The Amys approach. "You won't get us without a fight," she murmured under her breath a second later as the three girls swept by without even glancing her way.

III

"Okay," Amy said, looking around the crowded cafeteria. "I guess it's time to get everyone pumped up about tomorrow."

"Go for it," Aimee urged, and Mel nodded.

Amy jumped to her feet. "Hey, everybody!" she called. As usual everyone in the cafeteria quieted down immediately and turned to see what she wanted. She smiled. It was good to be an Amy.

She opened her mouth to speak. But someone else spoke up first.

"Hold it!" Carrie Mersel shouted. She hopped up from her seat by the window and waved her arms, causing the droopy black sleeves of her sweater to swing back and forth. "I'm sure you've got some *totally* important comments to make about the dress code at your little fashion party, Amy," she said. "But first, there's some breaking news I think everyone should know about."

"Extra! Extra! Read all about it!" Jordan Sullivan sang out, standing up from his seat beside Carrie. He was holding a stack of papers, which he began passing out to everyone.

Amy was more confused than angry.

What were these losers up to now? Even Sam didn't seem to know. When Amy glanced his way, he was staring at the paper Jordan had just handed him with a puzzled frown.

"What's your deal, Carrie?" Amy demanded loudly. "I'm trying to make an announcement here."

Carrie didn't answer. She had pulled another stack of papers out from under her chair and was rushing around the room, tossing stacks of them onto each table she passed. The cafeteria wasn't silent anymore. People were whispering and talking as they grabbed curiously for the papers.

"You might want to save your breath," Jordan said, stopping next to The Amys' table and handing her a paper from his stack.

Amy frowned and grabbed it. What was this all about? The paper had a big headline at the top and a couple of pictures in the middle. She scanned it quickly.

<u>Late-Breaking</u> <u>News</u> <u>Bulletin!</u>
Two fund-raisers go head-to-head on school grounds tomorrow afternoon. Which one will *you* attend? *You* have to decide!

Amy scowled as she saw the two large black-and-white images lined up side by side below the text. The left-hand side featured a line drawing of a pile of prizes, including all the things Sam had mentioned during his announcement that morning. The caption beneath it said Prizes Galore and Fun for Everyone at the Fair. On the right, with a caption reading Fashion Freaks on Parade, was a photo of The Amys.

Aimee gasped when she got a good look at the photo. "Ugh!" she cried. "Look what those jerks did to us!"

Mel put her head in her hands.

Amy was so furious that she couldn't speak for a moment. She recognized the photo—it was one she had run in the *Observer* just a couple of weeks ago. But someone had tampered with it. In a *big* way. Instead of the stylish outfits and cool hairstyles they had really been wearing when the picture was taken, The Amys appeared to be dressed like . . . like . . . like total nerds! No, worse than nerds— complete and utter freaks!

Aimee's jeans and crop top had been

replaced by a clown suit. Big, floppy red shoes poked out from under baggy, polka-dotted pants and a plaid shirt. A big red dot covered her nose. And her curly blond hair was now striped like a zebra.

As for Mel, she now appeared to be wearing geeky high-water slacks and a dorky ruffled pink blouse. A propeller cap was perched on her head. Her smooth dark hair had little yellow bows tied at the ends.

But Amy herself was the worst. Someone had decked her out in a complete Las Vegas–style sequin-and-rhinestone-encrusted powder blue jumpsuit. She looked like the flashiest, fattest, most ridiculous Elvis impersonator who ever lived. Her smiling blond head stuck out of the top of the mess, looking completely out of place.

It was obvious that some pinheaded computer geek had done this. He or she must have scanned the newspaper photo into a computer and added all that other stuff with a graphic design program. Just like those idiotic posters Sam had made up to advertise his fair.

All around her Amy could hear people starting to whisper and laugh. She felt her face turning bright red. Sam was behind this. Obviously. What was she going to do about it?

"So Amy," Carrie called out with a cocky grin. "Didn't you have some kind of announcement you wanted to make?"

Amy Anderson
<u>Notes</u> <u>to</u> <u>Myself</u>

I can't believe this is happening! How could I forget two of Daddy's most important rules of business?

Always know your audience.
Always know your enemies.

I didn't do so horribly on the first one. (Though maybe I should have realized that it would be easy for even a bunch of losers with a loser idea to talk the less fashion-forward elements at school out of coming to my show.) But it's the second one that's killing us now. I should have kept those nerds on the defensive! I could've done a lot more to sabotage the fair. Started more rumors. Made Sam and Co. look stupid in public. Figured out their plans and ruined them. It would have been so easy, and now it might be too late. I should have known that bunch of freaks wouldn't give up like normal people!

If I had totally destroyed this fair earlier on, one silly little piece of paper wouldn't be destroying my life!

But would-haves, could-haves, and should-haves aren't going to get me anywhere. So here's my new rule of life: <u>The</u> <u>show</u> <u>must</u> <u>go</u> <u>on!</u>

Eleven

"Yo, Sam," Brick called, loping across the field toward Sam and his friends. "Sorry we're late. Where should we set up?"

Sam grinned good-naturedly at the bus driver. It was funny—Brick looked a lot taller standing out here on the football field than he did hunched over the big steering wheel of bus number four. "Don't sweat it, bro," Sam assured him. "You're right on time. Or at least close enough for rock and roll."

Sam was feeling great. The fair had only started a little over an hour ago, and it was already a huge success. Sky was working at the admissions table, and she and the other volunteers could hardly pass out tickets and make change fast enough to keep up with demand. Everyone was here. Everyone. Middle schoolers. Parents. High schoolers and tiny tots. Even meatheaded jocks like Johnny Bates and Chris Tanzell had showed up. And more important, everyone—even the meatheads—seemed to be having a great time.

Sam pointed Brick toward the stage—really just an area near the goalpost marked out with wrestling mats—then went to check on the pony rides. Some of the volunteers had marked off a large ring behind the bleachers, and six or seven shaggy ponies were carrying small children around in circles, led by workers from Mrs. Mersel's country club. Sam immediately spotted Carrie standing next to her mother on the far side of the ring, looking grim and desperate. Then again, Carrie always looked grim and desperate when she had to spend any serious amount of time with her mother. Sam couldn't really blame her for that. If he had to live in the same house with Mrs. Mersel, he'd probably be feeling pretty grim and desperate himself before too long.

"Hi, Mrs. Mersel," he greeted the woman politely. He tried not to stare at the high-heeled pumps she was wearing. It had drizzled all night, and the shoes kept sinking into the damp ground. You could hardly even tell anymore that the aqua leather perfectly matched the color of Mrs. Mersel's crisp business suit. "Do you mind if I borrow Carrie for a while? Uh, I need her help with something."

"Of course, dear," Mrs. Mersel replied. "Everything is perfectly under control here."

"Thanks, I owe you a big one for rescuing me from her evil clutches," Carrie said when she and Sam were out of Mrs. Mersel's earshot. "You interrupted one of her patented speeches on being more organized and responsible." She grimaced. "I was getting ready to start a stampede just to shut her up. Those ponies are small, but I bet their hooves could do some damage."

Sam laughed. "Well, you're free now. For a while at least. Want to walk around with me?"

"Sure," Carrie said immediately. "I should check on the haunted house soon, anyway." She glanced around as the two of them wandered across the field toward the food tents. "You know, it's really kind of amazing that this all came together so well."

"It didn't just come together," Sam corrected. "We worked really hard. The five of us, and the vendors, and the other volunteers . . ."

Carrie held up her hand. "Don't launch into one of your political speeches, okay?" she joked. "You've already got my vote."

Sam chuckled. "Sorry," he said. "I guess this political stuff is kind of going to my head. It's just so cool that the fair is a success, you know? I mean, for a while there it was looking pretty grim." He cast her a sideways glance. "I wonder what did it. My stirring homeroom announcement? Or a certain last minute news flash?"

Carrie grinned. "No need to thank me," she said airily. "Jordan and I did that for the greater good of the student body. Or whoever it is you're always babbling about."

"Yeah, right," Sam said. "You did it to get back at The Amys."

"Okay, you know us too well." Carrie shrugged. "But we also did it to help a friend. Namely you. We didn't want you to be totally publicly humiliated." She grinned again. "After all, that could ruin our reputations. The Amys might not even talk to us anymore." She rolled her eyes. "By the way, I would just like to point something out. Dwight and his hacker buddies were really helpful and all, but you know I had to be desperate to agree to a plan that involved computers."

Sam knew that she was only partly kidding about that. "Right," he said. "Well, thanks. I guess." He wasn't sure what to think of what Carrie and Jordan had done. He'd wanted to take the high road in this battle with The Amys. But as he glanced around the busy fairgrounds he couldn't help wondering if making The Amys look bad had been the best way to go. If his friends hadn't stepped in, would all these people be here right now?

Carrie's attention had strayed from their conversation. They were approaching the dunking booth. "Uh-oh," she commented grimly. "It looks like all three of Jordan's Neanderthal older brothers are lined up to take a shot at dunking poor Alex. I'd better go bail her out. Literally, I mean."

"Cool," Sam said absently. He watched her hurry toward the dunking booth. Then he turned and wandered down a row of sideshow games. People were lined up three deep at every booth. Everyone was laughing, having fun . . . and spending money. That was the point of all this, wasn't it? To raise money for the school trip. What difference did it make how it had happened? Most people didn't really seem to care much about whether politicians played fair or took the high road. They cared about results. And Sam had really delivered the goods today.

So why did he have that slightly queasy feeling in the pit of his stomach?

He had to toughen up if he wanted to stick with this. Especially if he wanted to run for office someday when he was older.

He smiled at that thought. Ever since winning the election and becoming treasurer, he'd had a recurring daydream about his high-powered future political career. Okay, maybe he liked being in the background. But a guy could fantasize, couldn't he? The daydream varied a little each time. Sometimes he was a U.S.

senator, making important speeches on the Senate floor. Other times he was traveling to exotic places, rubbing elbows with world leaders as the newly appointed ambassador to France or Germany.

But his favorite version was when he pictured himself being interviewed on *NBC Nightly News*. It usually went something like this:

Tom Brokaw [jovially]: With me today is Samuel Jefferson Wells, the newly elected president of the United States. Sam, you won the election in the biggest landslide in history. How do you feel about that?

President Sam Wells [earnestly]: Hello, Tom. Thanks for having me on the show. To answer your question, I feel great. It just goes to show that if you work hard for everyone, the people will notice. That's what I've always tried to do ever since I won my first election as treasurer of Robert Lowell Middle School.

Tom Brokaw: Ah, yes, Robert

Lowell Middle School. I know it well. And now you've gone from Washington State to Washington, D.C.

As he strolled past the fortune-teller's tent Sam noticed that there was a long line snaking around the tent. Some of the people near the front of the line already had dollar bills in their hands, obviously waiting eagerly for their chance to hear what the future would bring them. Sam smiled and allowed himself to sink a little deeper into his daydream.

President Sam Wells: That's right, Tom. And I want the American people to know that I take my responsibility to them very seriously. I want to represent every person in this great nation—to be a voice of fairness and justice.
Tom Brokaw [leaning forward, with a predatory gleam in his eye]: That all sounds very impressive, Mr. President. But a reputable source tells

me that you may not have always lived up to those ideals in the past. I understand you once allowed your supporters to deviously, under-handedly, and unfairly sabotage a school fund-raiser—a fashion show—just to save yourself from a little embarrassment. How do you respond to these charges? And does this mean that you're prejudiced against the fashionable?

President Sam Wells [stammering]: Er, um, uh . . .

Tom Brokaw [going in for the kill]: I also understand, Mr. President, that your middle name isn't really Jefferson at all.

Whoa! Sam shook his head and snapped out of it. Okay, so *that* daydream had kind of gotten away from him. He was obviously feeling more than a little bit guilty about all this.

And he was starting to figure out why. This stupid battle of wills between himself and Amy shouldn't have started in the first place. He couldn't believe he'd so totally lost sight of what was important here. . . .

He turned and hurried back past the fortune-teller's tent, heading toward the school building. It was time for a real political showdown.

Amy Anderson:
Legislative Loser

SATURDAY . . . ONE HOUR BEFORE SHOW TIME. Amy, Aimee, and Mel are setting up in the auditorium. The clothes are there. The makeup is there. The models are starting to arrive. Amy sends Aimee out front to start selling tickets.

HALF AN HOUR BEFORE SHOW TIME. Amy goes out to see how the ticket sales are going. A few of the models' parents and siblings have showed up. Nobody else has bought a single ticket so far. The audience looks pathetically sparse. But it's still early. . . .

FIFTEEN MINUTES BEFORE SHOW TIME. Amy finishes getting dressed and goes up front again to sell tickets so Aimee can take her turn getting ready. By now the rest of the models' parents have arrived. But they're still the only ones in the audience.

FIVE MINUTES BEFORE SHOW TIME. Krysta Barton shows up at the ticket table, breathless. She reports that Sam's fair is in full swing. She even shows off the Seattle Supersonics T-shirt she won as a door prize. She hopes it won't distract any of the models if it glows in the dark while they're onstage. Amy grits her teeth and forces herself not to say something sarcastic. After all, Krysta wants to buy a ticket. And she's the only member of their audience so far who isn't related to any of the models.

SHOW TIME. Aimee and Mel come out front to see what Amy is doing. Amy is forced to tell them that she's sold only one ticket. Aimee suggests that everyone wants to be "fashionably late." Amy glares at her. This is a fine time for Aimee to develop a sense of humor! She decides to delay the start of the show to give people a little more time to show up.

116

TEN MINUTES PAST SHOW TIME. The models and their parents are getting restless. They want to get started. But Amy holds out grimly. Suddenly someone new shows up, slightly breathless. It's Lydia, the manager of Stylistics. She hopes she isn't too late to get a ticket for the show. . . .

FIFTEEN MINUTES PAST SHOW TIME. The models are really antsy by now. And Lydia is downright annoyed. She thought her clothes were going to be part of some kind of fabulous show. But no one is here! Amy is humiliated.

TWENTY MINUTES PAST SHOW TIME. Amy is ready to give up and start the show. It's clear that nobody else is going to come. Just then the last person she expects to see walks into the auditorium. Sam. He comes up to Amy and asks where everyone is. Amy accuses him of stealing her audience with his lame fair. They start to argue. But Sam stops. He says this is stupid. The whole point was to make money for the school. All this time they should have found a way to work together instead of against each other. He says he's going to fix that right now.

He grabs a startled Amy by the arm and drags her out of the auditorium.

Twelve

Amy had no idea what Sam was up to as he pulled her along behind him out of the auditorium and up toward the playing fields behind the school building. She scowled when she caught her first glimpse of the football field. Obviously his geeky fair was a complete success. Booths and tents crowded the field, with kids and adults packed into the spaces between them. What was wrong with all these people? How could they have walked right past her fashion show to come to *this*?

She let her gaze drift around the action-packed sight. Delicious smells wafted toward her from the closest group of food tents, carried by the slight breeze. Cheers rang out from the sideshow games and the dunking booth. People poured in and out of the fortune-teller's tent. Half a dozen ponies carried the smaller children around in a circle, seemingly oblivious to the pounding rhythm of Brick's band. For once even the unpredictable Pacific Northwest weather patterns were cooperating. There wasn't a drop of rain in sight.

For just a second Amy couldn't help thinking that it looked like fun. Then she caught herself and scowled harder than ever.

"If you just want to bring me out here and humiliate me, you can forget it," she snapped, wrenching her arm free of Sam's grasp. This had already been the worst day of her life. She wasn't about to let the likes of Sam Wells rub her nose in it.

Sam smiled and shrugged. "Hey, you don't have to come along," he said. "I just thought you might like to hear the announcement I'm about to make. You know, so you'd be prepared."

Amy frowned. That sounded kind of ominous to her. But before she could demand an explanation, Sam loped off toward the stage—if you could call it that—where the band was playing. Amy crossed her arms and waited. She figured she might as well stay and find out what Sam was up to now. It wasn't as though she was burning to return to the pathetic scene back in the auditorium.

The band finished a song with a crash of drums. Sam hopped up onto the stage and grabbed the microphone. "Thank you, Xenophobes!" he shouted to the band, clapping the lead singer on the shoulder. "Now listen up, everyone." His voice rang out over the entire field. "I hope you're all having fun. I've got an important announcement to make. One of the biggest and most exciting events of the day will be starting in the school auditorium in about fifteen minutes. It's a fashion show, run by our very own school president, Amy Anderson, and it's sure to be a blast. It costs a dollar extra, but as you all know, the money goes into our school trip fund. And I can guarantee you that you'll get your money's worth. So let's head on down!"

Amy's jaw dropped. Was she hallucinating?

Nope. She definitely wasn't. Seconds later a huge crowd of people was pushing past her, eager to get to the auditorium. Amy collected herself and shoved her way to the front of the crowd.

"Coming through," she sang out. "Right this way. You can buy your tickets at the table outside the door. No pushing! There's plenty of room for everyone!"

The fashion show was even more amazing than Amy had expected. The outfits looked fabulous, the music was perfect, and the audience was awed—especially when The Amys themselves pranced down the catwalk (well, okay, so it was really just the front part of the stage) for the grand finale.

But all too soon it was just about over. Amy joined hands with her friends and stepped to the edge of the stage to take their bows.

"We were awesome, you guys!" Aimee chattered excitedly as the thunderous applause washed over them.

"Totally," Mel agreed. "We were better than awesome. We were legendary."

Amy smiled and glanced out into the audience. Every seat was filled. There were even a few people standing at the back of the auditorium. This was great!

She stepped forward and raised both arms for silence. It took a while, but finally everyone quieted down.

"Thank you so much," she called to the crowd. "We really appreciate your kind and generous support. I'd like to take a moment right here and call the rest of the student council up on the stage with me."

Sam, who was sitting in the front row with his nerdy friends, looked surprised. Amy smiled at him encouragingly. After a moment he stood with a shrug and came forward. The class representatives followed him. Soon they were all standing beside Aimee and Mel on the stage behind Amy.

"That's better," she said sweetly. She gazed out over the audience again. "I just want all of you out there to know something. Even the best class president doesn't get very far without people to help her. And I certainly couldn't have made this day of fund-raising such a huge success without the support of these people standing right here. They were all just a tremendous help to me in planning the fair and this fashion show."

She glanced over her shoulder and saw

that Sam's jaw dropped in amazement. Amy tossed him a smirk. Then she turned back to the audience. "So let's have a big round of applause for my faithful helpers!" She started clapping enthusiastically.

Within seconds most of the spectators were clapping and cheering loudly. The only pockets of silence were on the stage behind her and in the front row, where Sam's friends sat agape and astounded.

Amy took a few steps back, clapping all the while, until she was standing next to Sam. She grinned and winked. "You didn't think I was going to let you take the credit for any of that, did you, Mr. Treasurer?" she whispered. "Oh, and by the way. I'll deny it if you ever try to quote me . . . but thanks for what you did up there."

She couldn't help laughing out loud at the expression on his face.

Life was good!

Thirteen

"A toast," Jordan sang out. He lifted his glass of ice water in Sam's direction. "To our fearless leader!"

Alex pounded her fists on the Formica-topped table in front of her, making her dish of lime sherbet jump. "Speech! Speech!" she cried.

Sam glanced up from his strawberry sundae and grinned. It was later that evening, and the five friends were gathered at their favorite local ice-cream parlor. "Thanks, guys," he said. "I couldn't have done it without all the little people, you know."

"Right," Carrie put in, stirring her chocolate soda. "Like Amy Anderson, for instance? Oh, or when you said little people, weren't you referring to the people with tiny brains?"

Sky rolled her eyes. "Let's not mention

The Amys, okay?" she begged. "This is supposed to be a festive occasion. The fair was a huge success."

"It was more than huge," Jordan protested. "It was tremendous. Gigantic. Colossal! A fair to end all fairs. A fair for the record books!"

"Okay, enough already," Sky said. She glanced at Sam over her tall banana smoothie. "So did Amy really thank you after the show?"

"I thought we weren't going to talk about The Amys," Alex protested.

"Get real," Carrie said. "What else are we going to talk about after that stunt Amy pulled?" She snorted. "What nerve! Taking credit for all Sam's hard work like that."

Sam could tell that Carrie was on the verge of working herself up into a real fury about this. He couldn't blame her too much. He'd been pretty mad himself at first. But by now he had put it all into perspective. After all, it was hardly the worst thing The Amys had ever done. It certainly wasn't the first time they'd totally hosed Sam or his friends. And it probably wouldn't be the last.

"Relax, Carrie," he soothed her. "It's no big deal. The important thing is that we raised a lot of money for the school's trip fund. It doesn't really matter who takes the credit for it."

"Of course it matters!" Jordan exclaimed. "Are you nuts, dude? She totally scammed you!"

"Not to mention the entire town," Alex put in dryly, reaching for a napkin. "Really, Sam. Doesn't it bother you even a little? You did all that work."

Sam shrugged. "Well, okay, maybe a little," he said. "But I've always been a behind-the-scenes guy, you know? I don't need all that public attention like she does."

He meant it, too. He'd learned his lesson—you couldn't let personal stuff get in the way of doing what you needed to do. That wasn't what public service was all about. It was about getting things done for people, not getting interviewed on *The Today Show*; about sticking with your promises, not getting your name in the newspaper. It was just too bad The Amys never seemed to learn that lesson. . . .

Suddenly a thought popped into Sam's mind. He glanced around at his friends, a mischievous twinkle lighting up his dark eyes. "For instance," he said, carefully enunciating each word, "I would never have written the kind of stuff they put in the *Observer* this week. *I* could never write a totally glowing article about myself. *I* wouldn't feel right about using the power of the press to influence people." He paused and took a sip of his water. "Besides, I'm not on the newspaper staff."

Alex looked puzzled, and Sky was playing with her straw and not paying much attention. But Carrie and Jordan exchanged a glance. Then they grinned.

"I guess you have a point," Carrie said casually. "After all, we wouldn't want you to stoop to their level. That just wouldn't be acceptable for an elected official. Right?"

Jordan nodded and leaned back in his seat. "Right."

"Right," Sam agreed.

Sam Wells's Political Diary

Dateline: Saturday, 11 p.m.

I think I'm finally really getting the hang of this political stuff!

Okay, maybe I'm not quite ready for the White House yet. Or Tom Brokaw, either; that dude can ask some pretty tough questions! But now I know I can handle Robert Lowell Middle School. Even our oh-so-esteemed president!

There are a few things I want to remember from this whole fund-raising gig. For one thing, I hope I'll never let stupid bickering and that kind of personal stuff make me forget why I wanted to be an officer again: to help my school. And next time I'll be sure to keep a closer eye on what The Amys are up to.

Oh, and one last thing: something all politicians should learn. Amy Anderson already knew it, and now I do, too.

Sometimes it really helps to have friends in the press!

SAM WELLS OFFERS SOMETHING FOR EVERYONE!

BY CARRIE MERSEL AND JORDAN SULLIVAN

Our school trip is saved! Give it up for the person who made it happen—the one and only Sam Wells!

We probably don't need to bother to report on the details of Sam's fund-raising extravaganza. There's hardly an *Observer* reader out there who didn't turn out for the fair—to win prizes, eat delicious food, enjoy exciting games and great music, and watch that fabulous fashion show.

And *none* of it could have happened without our dedicated, hardworking, humble school treasurer, Sam Wells.

"I'm a behind-the-scenes guy," Sam told us modestly. And it's true. Like the great leader he is, he was very generous about sharing credit for the success of the day with his many eager volunteers. But any astute observer could see that it was Sam and Sam alone who had the brains, talent, and energy to bring all the elements together. And why did he do it? Not for the glory. Not for any personal gain. No, he did it for the greater good of us all.

J. Sullivan

We hope you'll join us in thanking him. We suggest that each of you out there take a moment to stop Sam in the hall and let him know you appreciate what he's done for us.

While you're at it, you might also want to save a word or two of thanks for our school president and vice president, Amy Anderson and Aimee Stewart. We understand that they really were quite a big help with the tasks they took on under Sam's guidance. For instance, they used their considerable shopping skills to help make the arrangements to borrow the clothes for the centerpiece of Sam's fair, the fashion show. And they still found time to model, too! Well done, Amy and Aimee!

As for the rest of you, *fair*-well for now! See you on the school trip!

Collect all the titles in the
MAKING FRIENDS series!

The prices shown below are correct at the time of going to press.
However, Macmillan Publishers reserve the right to show new retail
prices on covers which may differ from those previously advertised.

All MAKING FRIENDS titles can be ordered at your
local bookshop or are available by post from:

**Book Service by Post
PO Box 29, Douglas, Isle of Man IM99 1BQ**

Credit cards accepted. For details:
Telephone: 01624 675137
Fax: 01624 670923
E-mail: bookshop@enterprise.net

Free postage and packing in the UK.
Overseas customers: add £1 per book (paperback)
and £3 per book (hardback).